VIZ GRAPHIC NOVEL

A TASTE OF REVENGE
Crying Freeman Graphic Novel

Part 2

STORY BY
KAZUO KOIKE

ART BY
RYOICHI IKEGAMI

CONTENTS

Story by Kazuo Koike
Art by Ryoichi Ikegami
★
English Adaptation/Will Jacobs
Touch Up Art & Lettering/Wayne Truman
Cover Design/Viz Graphics
Executive Editor/Seiji Horibuchi
Editor/Satoru Fujii
★
First Published by Shogakukan, Inc., in Japan
Editor-in-Chief/Yonosuke Konishi
Executive Editor/Katsuya Shirai
★
Published by Viz Communications, Inc.
P.O. Box 77010, San Francisco, CA 94107.
★
10 9 8 7 6 5 4 3 2 1
First Printing January 1993

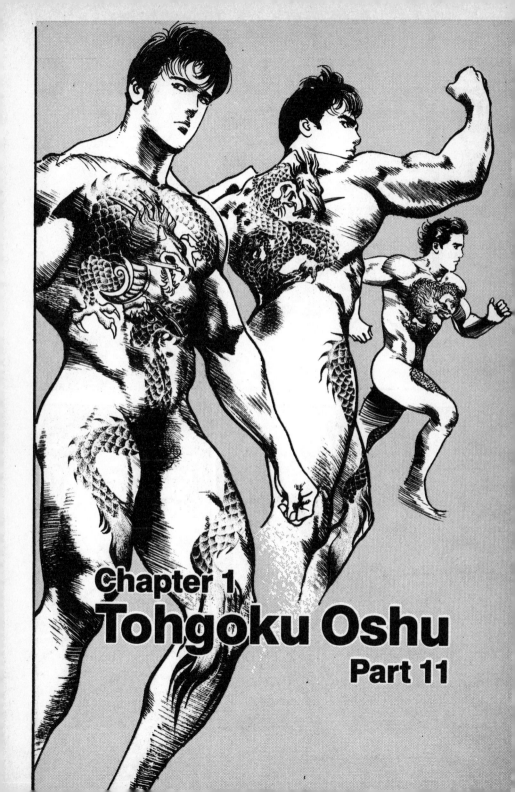

Chapter 1
Tohgoku Oshu
Part 11

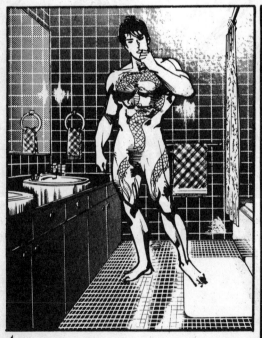

4

I NEVER EXPECTED THAT WE WOULD CAPTURE THE ORIGINAL SO EASILY. AND ALIVE, AT THAT.

IT WAS WISE TO RECRUIT MEN BUILT LIKE FREEMAN AND HAVE THEM SIMILARLY TATTOOED. I KNEW THAT THEY WOULD BE USEFUL SOMEDAY.

THE CREDIT GOES TO KIMIE.

SHE DELIVERED HIM TO US BEFORE OSHU COULD KILL HIM.

THE DATA ON FREEMAN THAT NITTA PROVIDED PROVED VERY ACCURATE.

HERE IS YOUR REWARD?

ONE HUNDRED MILLION YEN. SPEND IT WISELY.

OHH

THE DOUBLES MUST COPY FREEMAN'S EVERY MOVE AND HABIT TO A FAULT.

BUT THERE MUST BE A FALSE MOVEMENT OR TWO SO THAT WE WILL BE ABLE TO DISTINGUISH THEM.

MOST IMPORTANTLY, WE MUST LEARN ALL HIS SEXUAL HABITS.

HOW DOES FREEMAN MAKE LOVE TO HIS WIFE?

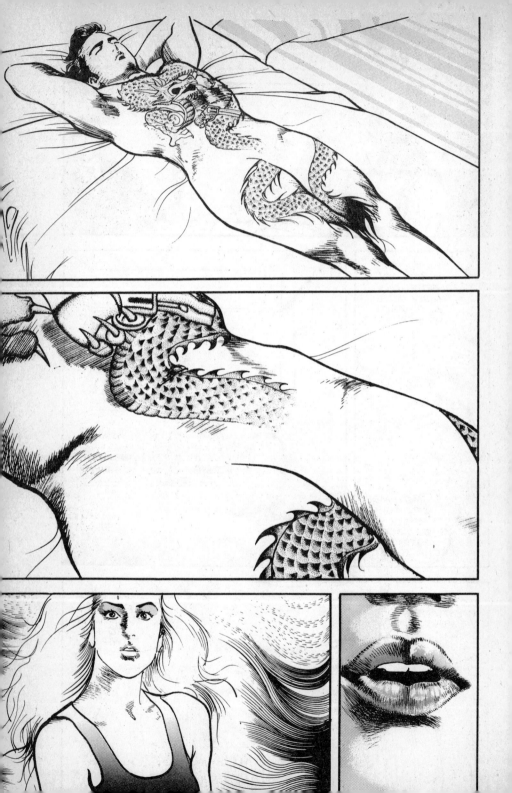

THE HEAD OF HIS PENIS IS THICKER THAN NORMAL. I DETECT NO OTHER PECULIARITIES.

IT'S OF AN AVERAGE LENGTH, I WOULD SAY.

WE'VE DRUGGED HIM TO ACCEPT OUR SUBLIMINAL SUGGESTIONS. FORTY MINUTES AGO, WE GAVE HIM A POWERFUL LOVE POTION AND A SLEEPING PILL.

LOOK. ALREADY HIS PENIS SWELLS.

KIMIE.

YES.

YOU WILL SLEEP WITH FREEMAN AND LEARN EVERY ASPECT OF HIS SEXUAL BEHAVIOR.

DON'T MISS A SINGLE DETAIL.

MASTER NAIJI! KIMIE IS...

YOU ARE A MEDIOCRE MAN.

SELLING YOUR WIFE TO A WHOREHOUSE WAS CONSIDERED A VIRTUE IN THE DAYS OF OLD.

B-B-BUT...

BE MORE HARD-HEARTED, NITTA. FORGET EMOTION. BECOME AN OGRE OF REVENGE AGAINST FREEMAN.

KIMIE.

YES...

YOU MAY GIVE YOURSELF UP TO PLEASURE WITH FREEMAN. BUT MAKE SURE HE ENJOYS IT, TOO.

THE STRONGER HIS PLEASURE, THE MORE FULLY HE WILL EXPRESS HIS SEXUAL HABITS.

11

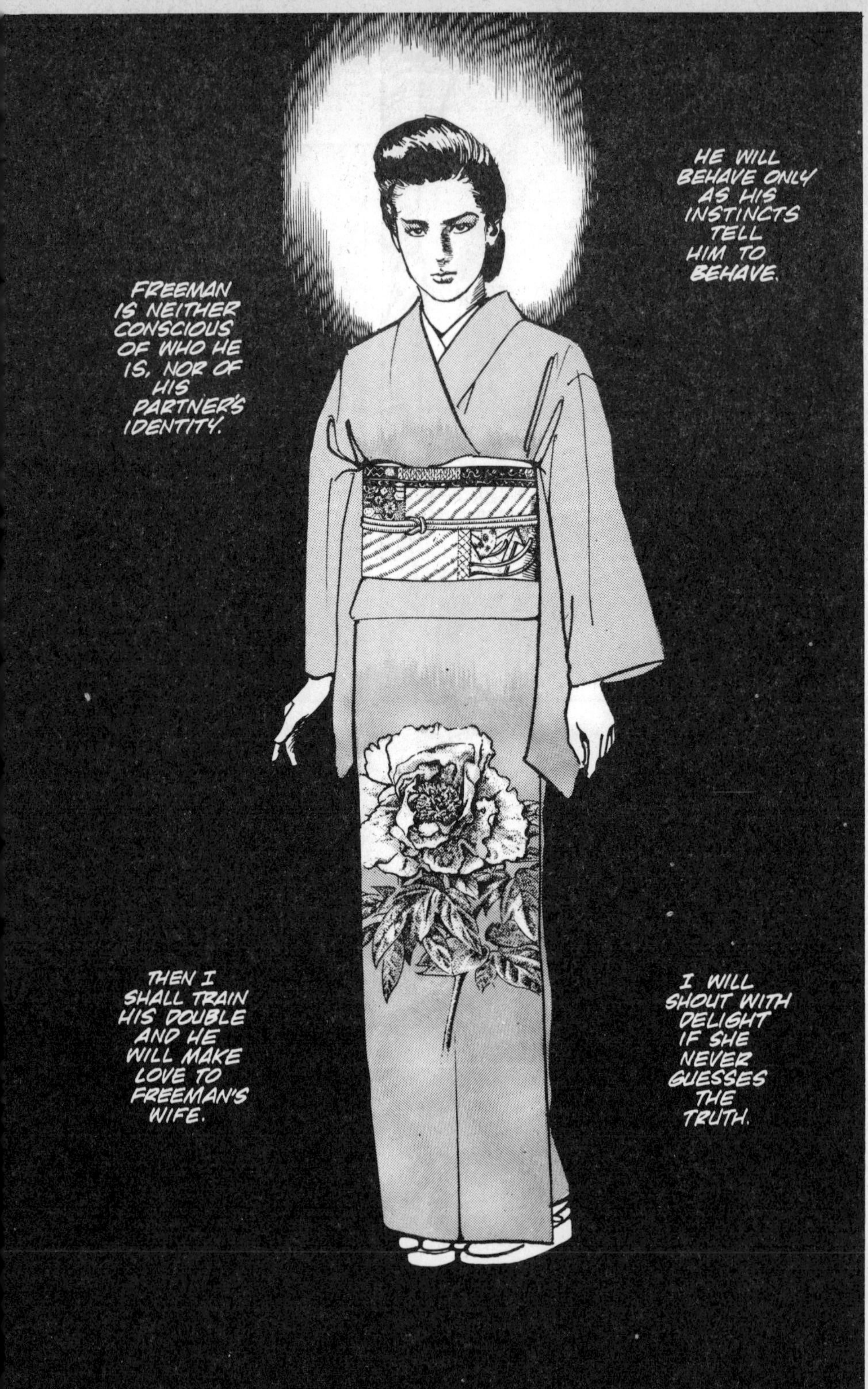
HE WILL BEHAVE ONLY AS HIS INSTINCTS TELL HIM TO BEHAVE.
FREEMAN IS NEITHER CONSCIOUS OF WHO HE IS, NOR OF HIS PARTNER'S IDENTITY.
THEN I SHALL TRAIN HIS DOUBLE AND HE WILL MAKE LOVE TO FREEMAN'S WIFE.
I WILL SHOUT WITH DELIGHT IF SHE NEVER GUESSES THE TRUTH.

WHO WOULD BELIEVE THAT IT'S A DOUBLE IF HIS OWN WIFE CAN'T TELL THE DIFFERENCE?

A LIE BECOMES A TRUTH IF WE STICK TO THE LIE FOREVER.

OUR TASK IS TO MAKE SURE THAT HIS WIFE NEVER KNOWS THAT SHE'S WITH A DOUBLE.

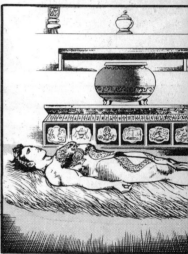

SHH SHH

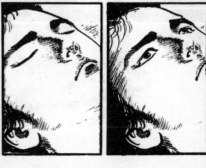

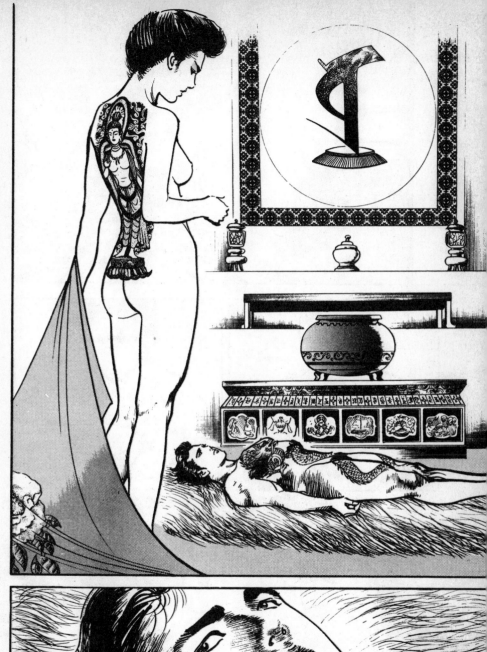

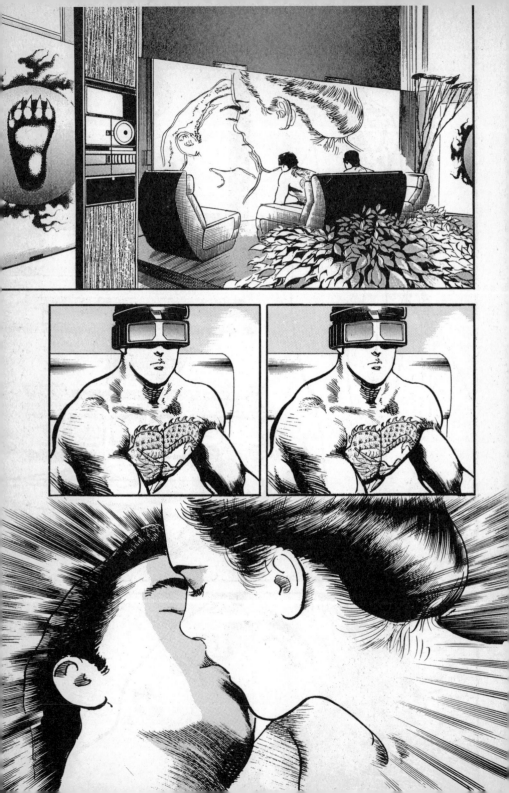

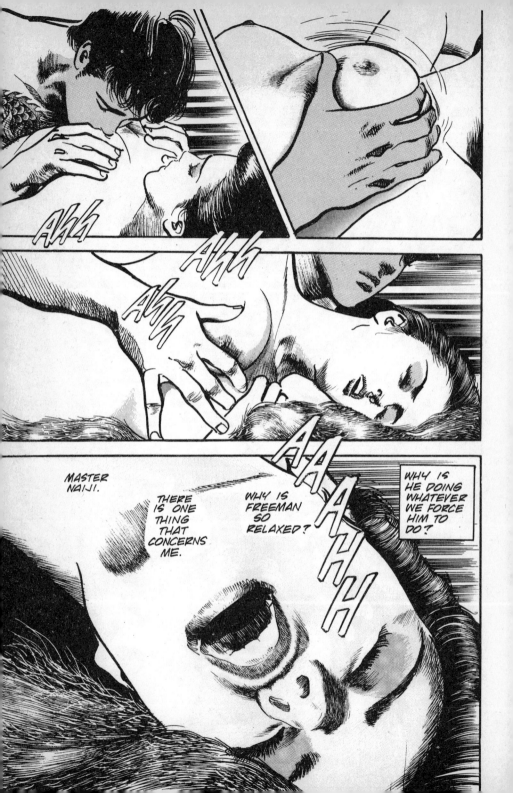

YOU ARE NO DOUBT CORRECT THAT HE IS HELPLESS IN OUR POWER...

BUT I AM STILL CONCERNED.

Chapter 1
Tohgoku Oshu
Part 12

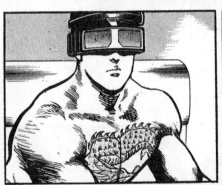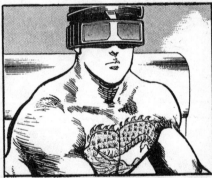

Uh...

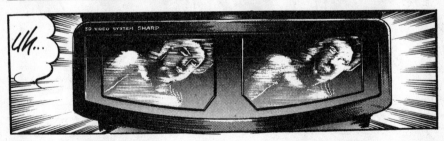

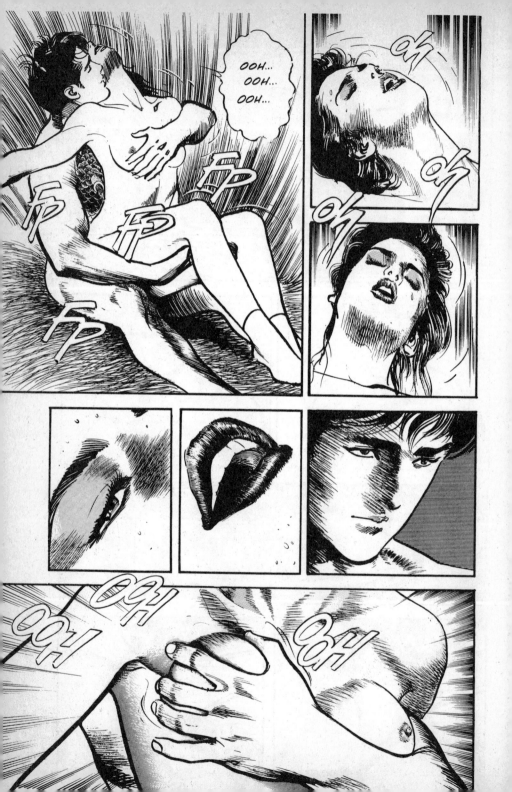

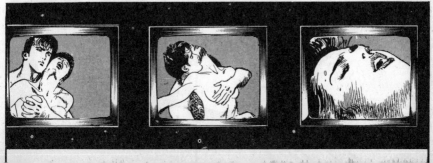

HOW CAN HE LAST SO LONG? IT'S BEEN OVER AN HOUR.

.....

GRR
GRR
GRR

KIMIE'S REALLY TURNED ON! DAMN IT!

mmf
mmf
mmf
mmf
mmf

SLRP
SLRP

SLp SLp
SLP
SLP
SLp

OH... SO
GOOD...
SO
GOOD...

OHHHHHHHH!

GULP

DAMN!

WHA-? THAT... THAT BASTARD!

NO!

NO! DON'T!

DID YOU FORGET WHAT I TOLD YOU, NITTA, ABOUT BECOMING AN OGRE?

IF YOU WANT REVENGE ON FREEMAN, YOU MUST HARDEN YOUR HEART!

B-B-BUT...

uqhh... uqhh...

FREEMAN IS SUPPRESSING A DEEP PSYCHOLOGICAL WOUND.

IT SHOWS UP WHEN HE CRIES AFTER HE HAS KILLED. AND IT'S SHOWING UP NOW, IN HIS SEXUAL PERFORMANCE.

WHEN A SUPPRESSED PERSON SEEKS TO FREE HIS SPIRIT, HE ENDS UP A SADIST OR A MASOCHIST.

SEXOLOGISTS HAVE LONG HELD THIS THEORY.

WATCH VERY CAREFULLY!

ULP

whew

OHHHH

UH...
UH...
UH...

THAT WAS INCREDIBLE...

I CAME FIVE TIMES...

AND YET I THOUGHT HE WAS REALLY GOING TO KILL ME...

Z₂Z
ZZ²
Z₂Z

BUT... WHY WAS HE SO CALM...?

HE WAS COOL, SELF-POSSESSED, THE WHOLE TIME... EVEN WHEN HE WAS STRANGLING ME.

I'M SCARED...

AND WHY DIDN'T HE COME? AFTER ALL THAT TIME?

SO, IT SEEMS THAT YOU'VE LEARNED EVERYTHING YOU WANTED.

NOW, WILL YOU GIVE HIM TO ME AS YOU PROMISED, MASTER NAJI?

NO. I'M NOT YET DONE WITH HIM.

WHAT? WHY?

WE MUST KNOW EVERYTHING ABOUT HIM IF THE DOUBLES ARE TO BE PERFECT.

WE MUST GRILL KIMIE ON EVERY DETAIL OF HIS LOVE MAKING. WE MUST KNOW HIS EVERY SEXUAL PATTERN.

IF NECESSARY, KIMIE MIGHT HAVE TO SLEEP WITH HIM AGAIN.

WHAT?!

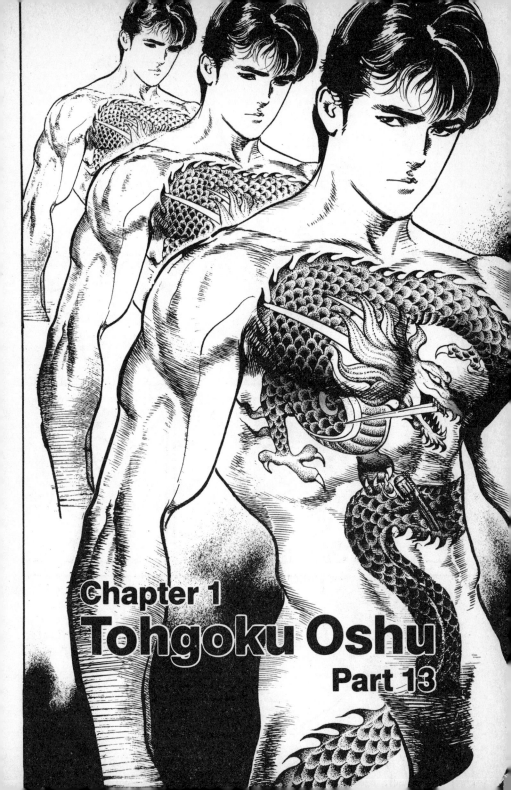

Chapter 1
Tohgoku Oshu
Part 13

COME IN. IT'S OPEN.

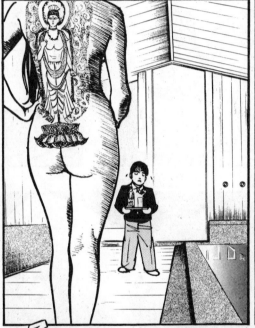

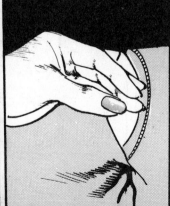

OHH

I'LL DO IT AGAIN FOR YOU IF YOU KEEP IT A SECRET.

YES, MA'AM.

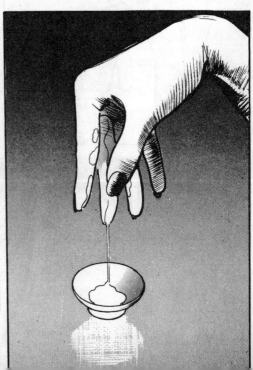

HMM. YOUTHFUL SEED.

GLP

43

44

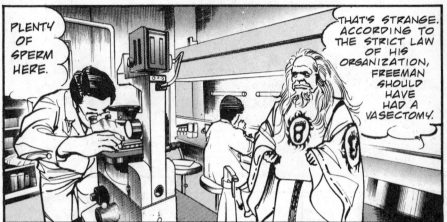

PLENTY OF SPERM HERE.

THAT'S STRANGE. ACCORDING TO THE STRICT LAW OF HIS ORGANIZATION, FREEMAN SHOULD HAVE HAD A VASECTOMY.

I WONDER.

THERE IS NO DOUBT THAT THIS SPERM CAME FROM FREEMAN...

PERHAPS HE HAS NOT HAD THE VASECTOMY YET.

IT BOTHERS ME. SHOULD I HAVE KIMIE GET ANOTHER SAMPLE FROM HIM?

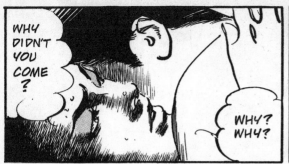

WHY DIDN'T YOU COME?

WHY? WHY?

YOU'RE MAKING ME LOSE FACE... AS A WOMAN.

I'M GONNA MAKE HIM COME IF IT TAKES ME ALL DAY. DAMN HIM!

SLRP

SLRP

SLRP

YES! KIMIE IS AFLAME WITH PASSION. HA HA HA HA HA HA

IT IS SAID THAT THERE IS NO LIMIT TO A WOMAN'S DESIRE.

NOW, I BELIEVE IT.

AND I WONDER HOW LONG FREEMAN CAN TAKE IT.

HOW DO YOU DO IT?

YOU DON'T COME, AND YET YOU'RE SO RELAXED.

I WONDER IF THE LOVE POTION IS WORKING.

ARE YOU DEAF? ANSWER ME.

I HAD TO PRETEND TO SWALLOW YOUR COME SO THAT THEY WOULDN'T KNOW THAT I'D FAILED AGAIN.

WHAT IS THE MATTER, KIMIE? THE DOUBLE DOES NOT EXCITE YOU AS MUCH AS FREEMAN HIMSELF?

Thp

I'M SORRY. IT FEELS STRANGE.

AHH

BUT...IT'S PROBABLY ALL IN MY MIND. I THINK I COULD GET INTO IT IF I DIDN'T KNOW IT WAS A DOUBLE.

THIS ONE RESEMBLES FREEMAN MORE THAN THE OTHER DOUBLE. THE FEELING WHEN HE IS INSIDE ME HITS CLOSER TO THE MARK.

MY MIND IS MADE UP.

NUMBER TWO.

BUT IT'S STILL DIFFERENT. I JUST CAN'T SEEM TO GET AROUSED...

YES, SIR.

YOU WILL BECOME FREEMAN FROM NOW ON.

AS YOU WISH, SIR.

NOW IT'S MY TURN.

KRK KRK

MASTER NAIJI.

WHAT IS IT?

THERE IS ONE THING THAT DISTURBS ME.

PLEASE, LET ME GO TO FREEMAN ONE MORE TIME.

HIS BREATH HAD A STRANGE ODOR. IT SMELLED LIKE...

I'M NOT SURE WHAT IT WAS. I'D LIKE TO CHECK IT AGAIN.

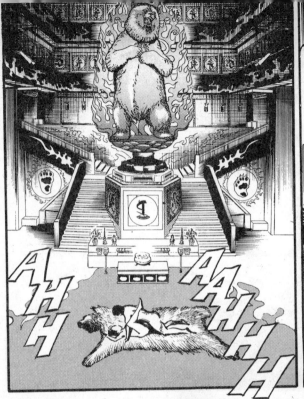

YOU WILL BE KILLED WHEN THIS IS OVER...

LET YOURSELF COME. THIS IS THE LAST CHANCE YOU'LL EVER HAVE.

LEAVE ME SOMETHING OF YOURS... YOUR SPERM...

LEAVE ME YOUR SELF.

WE'RE BEING WATCHED.

IF YOU DON'T COME, I'LL HAVE TO PUT YOU IN MY MOUTH AND PRETEND TO SWALLOW AGAIN.

PLEASE...

OH!

53

THRRRRRRNG

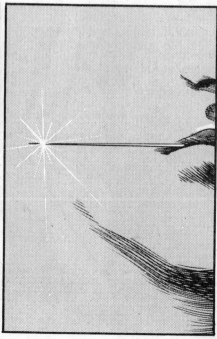

Chapter 1
Tohgoku Oshu
Part 14

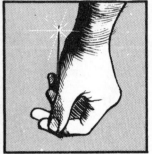

NUMBER TWO.

YES, SIR.

PUT ON SOME CLOTHES WHEN YOU WALK AROUND.

BUT, SIR. YOU HAVE TOLD ME TO DO AS FREEMAN WOULD DO, DOWN TO EVERY DETAIL.

YES, YOU ARE RIGHT.

HA!

NO. OPEN ME GENTLY.

YES, THAT'S THE PLACE...

NOW HARDER. USE ANOTHER FINGER, TOO...

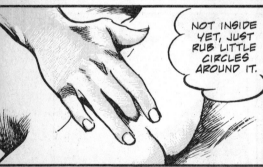

NOT INSIDE YET, JUST RUB LITTLE CIRCLES AROUND IT.

AHH

THMMP

DETAIN ANYBODY WHO COMES BY.

THRRRRRRNG-

WHAT ARE YOU DOING HERE?

WOULD YOU HOLD THIS CHECK FOR ME?

HMM.

GIVE ME A CIGARETTE.

CLICK

AFTER ALL I'VE HAD, YOU'RE STILL THE BEST.

I'M SCARED. YOU WILL PROTECT ME, WON'T YOU?

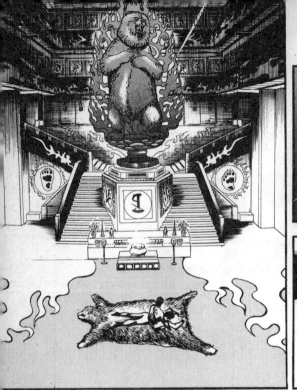

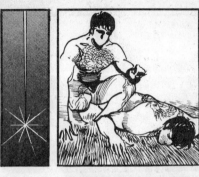

I HAVE TAKEN YOUR VOICE AWAY. YOU MUST FIGHT, IF YOU WANT TO LIVE.

THE DRAGON TATTOO YOU WEAR MEANS "FIGHT FOR FREEDOM."

65

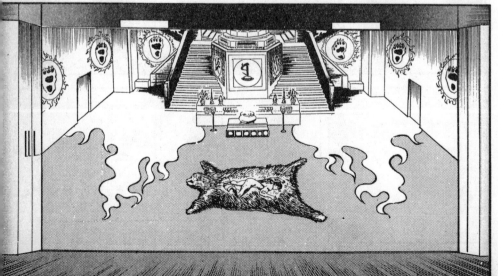

WHAT REMAINS TO BE DONE?

NOTHING, SIR.

NOW, THE NEW OM THAI YEUNG WILL RISE LIKE THE SUN, WILL RISE LIKE A DRAGON.

GRRR

YOU! ATONE FOR YOUR SINS, AND RETURN TO THE SOIL!

Heh

IT IS SAD THAT EVEN FREEMAN, WHO IS SAID TO BE A COOL KILLING MACHINE, CANNOT FACE UP TO HIS OWN DEATH.

UPON SEEING HIS MORTUARY TABLET, HE KNOWS FEAR... LOSES HIS POISE.

BUT AFTER ALL, HE IS SO YOUNG.

HE GOES TO EXTREMES, DOESN'T HE?

73

Chapter 2
Nothing Ventured,
Nothing Gained
Part 1

BY ANNEXING THE ORGANIZATION OF THE 108 DRAGONS, WE WILL BECOME THE MOST POWERFUL SYNDICATE IN THE WORLD.

O GOD OF THE GREAT BEAR, AID US WITH YOUR DIVINE PROVIDENCE.

GRROWWW

CRKL CRKL

HUH?

THE GOD OF THE GREAT BEAR HAS SENT HIS EMISSARY. STEP FORWARD, NEWBORN FREEMAN.

DO YOU EXPECT TO PASS FOR THE LEADER OF THE 108 DRAGONS BY BEHAVING LIKE A COWARD?

YOU ARE NOW OM THAI YEUNG! ACT LIKE HIM!

THUP

TP

TP

TP

OHH!

NEVER DISOBEY ME, FREEMAN.

NEVER FORGET YOUR DUTY.

NEVER LOSE YOUR RESPECT FOR THE GOD OF THE GREAT BEAR.

SHH SHH

NEVER, SIR.

GOOD, GOOD. YOU LEAVE FOR HONG KONG IMMEDIATELY.

JAPAN AIR LINES

RRRRRR

SPLSSH

I WONDER IF SOMETHING HAS HAPPENED TO MY BROTHER.

HE PROMISED TO RETURN ON THIS, THE TWENTIETH DAY.

YES.

WE WILL WAIT ANOTHER DAY, BUT NO MORE. I PROMISED MY HUSBAND WE WOULD NOT LINGER IF HE WAS LATE.

BUT...

WE WILL GO HOME FOR NOW AND COME BACK LATER.

WE MUST SAY FAREWELL TO DRAGON FATHER AND TIGER MOTHER AND TAKE STEPS TO SECURE THE FUTURE OF OUR ORGANIZATION. AFTER THAT WE WILL RETURN.

YES.

WE'RE GOING HOME.

YES, MA'AM.

SPLSSH

HELLO, PROFESSOR MIKAGE.

A FORTUITOUS COINCIDENCE HAS BROUGHT US TOGETHER. HAD FU CHING LAN NOT BEEN YOUR STUDENT, I MIGHT NOT HAVE GAINED CONTROL OF THE 108 DRAGONS.

CLP CLP

TEN MILLION YEN. I WISH I COULD OFFER YOU MORE.

Ahh

IT'S BEEN TWO YEARS SINCE YOU LOST YOUR WIFE, HASN'T IT?

I THINK YOU NEED A YOUNG WOMAN TO LOOK AFTER YOU. WHAT DO YOU THINK OF HER?

Hmm

I AM AYA TAKEMI, MY LORD.

I'LL TAKE HER!

THEN IT WENT WELL?

NOW WE ARE ALL FORTUNATE THAT ONE OF YOUR STUDENTS MARRIED OM THAI YEUNG.

FOR HAD YOU NOT PROVIDED ME WITH SO MUCH INFORMATION, WE COULD NEVER HAVE TRAINED A DOUBLE SO THOROUGHLY.

SO WELL THAT THE REAL OM THAI YEUNG NO LONGER EXISTS IN THIS WORLD.

AND ONE OF OUR DOUBLES IS HEADING FOR HONG KONG RIGHT NOW. HA HA HA HA HA HA!

HE POSSESSES EVERY SHRED OF KNOWLEDGE YOU GAVE US ABOUT FREEMAN.

FIRST I SENT KAIEDA WITH THE EVIL SWORD, MURAMASA. THEN YOU.

OUR PLAN WAS A COMPLETE SUCCESS. HA HA HA HA!

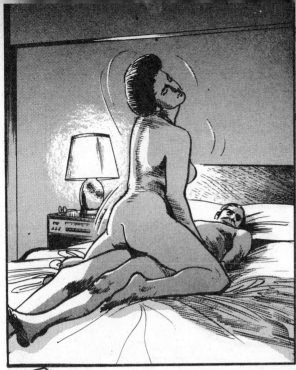

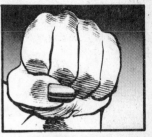

THANK YOU FOR THE WELCOME.

Chapter 2
Nothing Ventured, Nothing Gained
Part 2

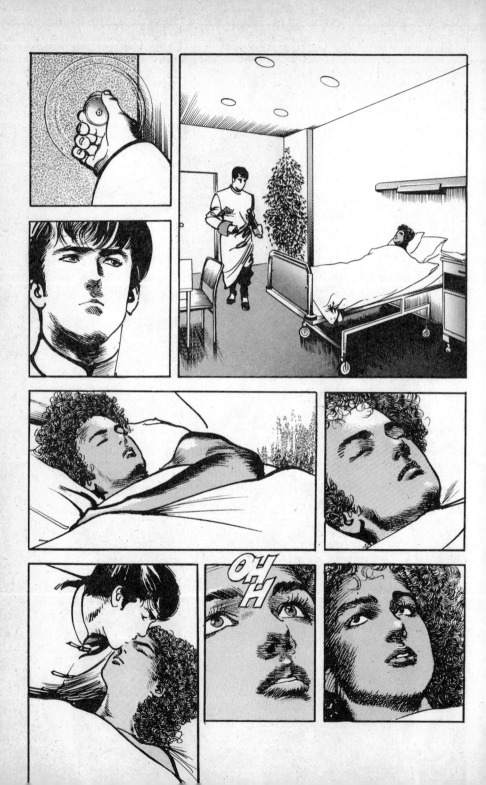

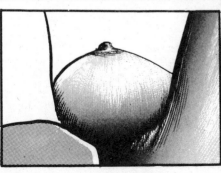

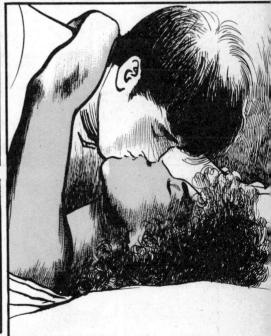

YOU'RE DOING SPLENDIDLY, COPYMAN.

SHHHH. THE WALLS HAVE EARS.

I DIDN'T EXPECT YOU TO CARRY IT OFF SO WELL. I'M IMPRESSED.

YOU LOOK JUST LIKE THE REAL FREEMAN. YOU ACT JUST LIKE HIM, EVEN DOWN TO THE AIR OF DIGNITY. AND BEST OF ALL, NOBODY DOUBTS YOU.

YOU ARE TO BE COMMENDED.

BEEP

WHAT IS IT ?

LADY FU CHING LAN IS ON HER WAY HOME.

SHE WILL ARRIVE WITHIN SIX HOURS.

THE TIME HAS COME.

FU CHING LAN WILL SOON MEET HER "HUSBAND."

IF SHE SEES THROUGH HIS ACT, WE WON'T GET OUT OF HERE ALIVE.

99

SPLSSH

BROTHER!

DEAR.

WHAT HAPPENED, BROTHER?

LET ME INTRODUCE OUR GUESTS.

MR. NITTA, MR. TOHGOKU OSHU...

...AND MISS KIMIE HANADA.

EXCELLENT.

I DIDN'T DO ANYTHING. MURAMASA DOES IT FOR ME.

THEN, MURAMASA MUST HAVE ACCEPTED YOU AS ITS MASTER.

AND IT'S ACCEPTED YOU, TOO.

AS MY HUSBAND.

MURAMASA KNOWS THAT I WOULD BE SAD IF YOU GOT HURT.

THAT'S WHY IT DOESN'T CUT THE FLOWER.

IF MURAMASA HAD CUT THE FLOWER, IT WOULD HAVE SOUGHT YOU OUT AS ITS NEXT TARGET.

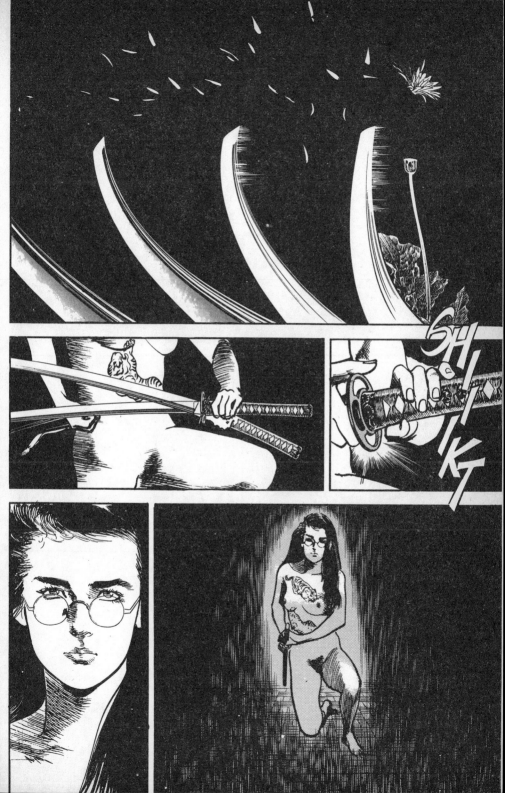

DARLING
!

OH,
OH,
OH,
OHHH...

KREEK.

KREEK.

KREEK.

KREEK.

KREEK

WHAT THE HELL'S WRONG, KIMIE? YOU'RE A MILLION MILES AWAY!

WE WON'T SURVIVE IF FU CHING LAN SEES THROUGH THE DECEPTION.

HOW COULD I GET HOT AT A TIME LIKE THIS?

WE'LL WORRY ABOUT IT WHEN IT HAPPENS, DAMN IT!

SHE IS SO VERY, VERY BEAUTIFUL. BUT AFTER ALL, DOES A MAN LIKE FREEMAN DESERVE LESS?

HOW...HOW COULD I HAVE EVER HOPED TO COMPETE?

WELL! IT LOOKS LIKE WE'VE MADE IT!

HE MUST HAVE WORKED AWFULLY HARD TO SATISFY FU CHING LAN. HEH HEH HEH...

110

EVERYTHING'S FINE. HIS WIFE, THE ENTIRE ORGANIZATION-- THEY'VE ALL FALLEN FOR HIS FLAWLESS PERFORMANCE.

IT'S TIME YOU JOINED US.

GOOD. GOOD. HA HA HA HA!

HA HA HA HA HA HA!

111

Chapter 2
Nothing Ventured, Nothing Gained
Part 3

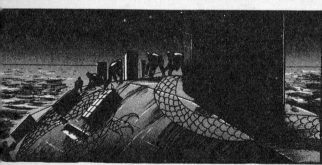

RRRRRRR

HA HA HA HA!
WE WILL TRANS-
PORT THE MODEL-
100 SUBMACHINE
GUNS INTO THE
HEADQUARTERS
OF THE 108
DRAGONS USING
THEIR OWN
SUBMARINE.

IT IS ALL
SO VERY
EASY, ISN'T
IT, MR.
IMAIDA
?

S—R—P

115

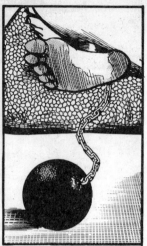

AFTER TRAINING THERE, OUR FORCES WILL CROSS THE SEA TO JAPAN ON THAT VERY SAME SUBMARINE. ANYWHERE FROM FIVE HUNDRED TO A THOUSAND MEN.

A WAVE OF TRAINED KILLERS...

...EACH ONE ARMED WITH A MODEL-100 SUBMACHINE GUN.

SUCH A CONQUEST OF JAPAN WILL BE A SIMPLE MATTER. WHAT DO YOU THINK?

I THINK YOU'RE CRAZY.

WELL, DRINK UP, ANYWAY.

AYA, POUR HIM SOME SAKE.

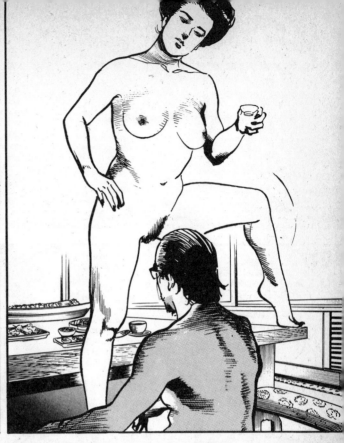

HA HA HA
HA HA
HA

THEN IN JAPAN TEN THOUSAND FOLLOWERS OF KUMAGAISM WILL RISE UP IN REVOLT.

WHY DON'T YOU COOPERATE, IMAIDA? USE YOUR AUTHORITY AS THE CHAIRMAN OF THE FEDERATION OF ECONOMIC ORGANIZATIONS FOR ME...

AND GET US MORE GUNS. YOU WERE ONCE THE HEAD OF PRODUCTION, AFTER ALL.

YOU CAN SPEARHEAD A PROJECT TO MANUFACTURE THOUSANDS OF THEM.

I WILL MAKE YOU MY PRIME MINISTER.

118

JUST KILL ME QUICKLY!

FIRST ANSWER A QUESTION. WHY STOCKPILE A THOUSAND SUBMACHINE GUNS ALL THESE YEARS?

I HOPED THAT THEY WOULD BENEFIT JAPAN SOMEDAY.

OH! YOU WERE RIGHT!

AND THE TIME IS... NOW!

YOU STINK! I SMELL BLOOD!

RRRRR~

SPLSSSSH

HA!

HMM

MASTER NAIJI! EVERYTHING IS GOING EXACTLY AS PLANNED.

WE CAME TO WELCOME YOU, GRANDPA.

YES, YES. BUT TELL ME, WHO IS THIS ENORMOUS WOMAN?

SHE IS IVORY FAN, THE SISTER OF OM THAI YEUNG.

YES, YES. THANK YOU.

HA HA HA HA.

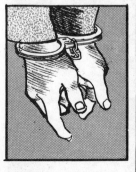

DID OM THAI YEUNG TELL YOU TO ADDRESS ME AS GRANDPA?

THAT'S RIGHT.

YES, YES.

WELCOME, MASTER NAIJI KUMAGA, MR IMAIDA.

FREEMAN...

YOU NEED NOT SPEAK, IMAIDA. I UNDERSTAND EVERYTHING.

PLEASE COME THIS WAY. I WELCOME YOU TO OUR HEADQUARTERS.

125

WHA-?!
WHAT
ARE YOU
DOING
?!

WHOOSH!

YOU!!

YOU BETRAYED ME !!

THERE HAS BEEN NO BETRAYAL. I AM THE **REAL CRYING FREEMAN.**

SLP

Chapter 2
Nothing Ventured,
Nothing Gained
Part 4

DID YOU KILL YOUR DOUBLE?

KRNCH

TOHGOKU OSHU HAD THAT PRIVILEGE.

THEN... THEN THAT WASN'T YOU?

BUT...HOW DID YOU MAKE THE SWITCH?

NO!

NOT KIMIE! SHE WOULDN'T HAVE...

NO! NO! NO!

BUT...
BUT...

BUT THE SLEEPING PILLS, AND THE APHRODISIACS SHE GAVE YOU...

FOR TWO THOUSAND YEARS THE 108 DRAGONS HAVE REFINED THE USE OF HERBS.

I SIMPLY TOOK THOSE THAT WOULD COUNTERACT YOUR POISONS.

L-LOOK!

LOOK AT THE DECORATIONS FOR OUR WELCOME.

THEY ARE ALL FUNERAL ORNAMENTS.

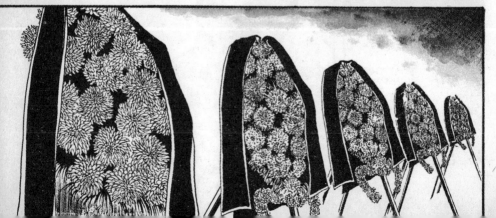

KIMIE! WAS IT REALLY YOU WHO BETRAYED US?!

KIMIE!

KLK KLK

HELP US! HELP US!

BRING MR. IMAIDA.

HERE HE IS.

WHUP

DAMN IT! BACK OFF!

TAKE US BACK TO JAPAN, OR HE DIES.

WHAT KIND OF POLICE DETECTIVE ARE YOU?

MR. IMAIDA...

THANK YOU.

OHH

OSHU! YOU'RE NOT GOING TO BETRAY ME TOO, ARE YOU?

I WISH ONLY TO FIGHT FREEMAN. ONE ON ONE.

OSHU, YOU KNEW IT WASN'T ME WHEN YOU KILLED THE DOUBLE.

OF COURSE. THAT MAN WAS NOT PREPARED TO DIE. I SAW ONLY TERROR IN HIS EYES.

YOU AND I HAVE FOUGHT MANY TIMES...

...BUT I HAVE SEEN ONLY SADNESS IN YOURS.

THE SADNESS YOU FEEL WHENEVER YOU MUST TAKE A LIFE.

YOU DUMB FOOL!

YOU CAME HERE WILLINGLY, KNOWING OUR CAUSE WAS BETRAYED?

FREEMAN BRAVED OUR LAIR WITH EMPTY HANDS.

HE CAME ALONE, WITHOUT WEAPONS.

OUR FIGHT WAS UNFAIR. HE WAS UNDER TOO GREAT A DISADVANTAGE.

THAT IS WHY I AM HERE NOW. TO FIGHT HIM ON EQUAL TERMS.

YOU ARE A COMPLETE FOOL!

HA HA!

HA HA HA HA HA!

HA HA HA HA HA!

144

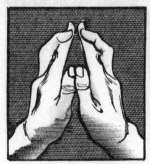

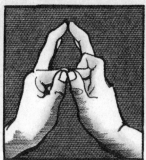

AH! HE'S CHANTING THE NINE-LETTER CURSE OF THE BEAR!

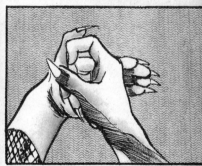

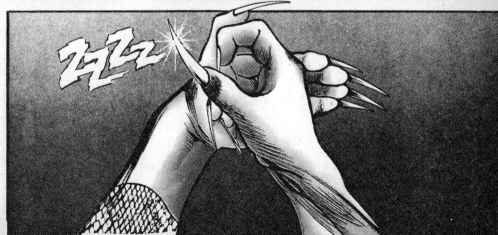

HE'S USING HYPNOTISM!

Chapter 2
Nothing Ventured, Nothing Gained
Part 5

RIN...PYO...
TOH...
SHA...KAI...

JIN...
RETU...ZAI...
ZEN!

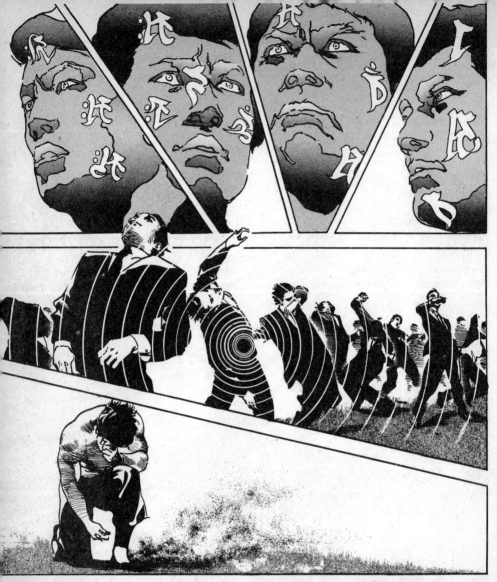

RIN...PYO...
TOH...SHA...
KAI... JIN...
RETU...
ZAI...ZEN!

154

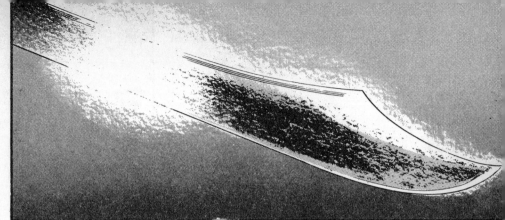

RIN...PYO...
TOH...SHA...
KAI...JIN...
RETU...
ZAI...ZEN!

WHEE

WHEE

Wha-?

ARRR...

CHIK

MURAMASA, THE EVIL SWORD!!

TKK

THMP

162

AS YOU WISH, OSHU.

LET US FIGHT TO THE DEATH, FREEMAN. IF I WIN, ALLOW ME TO RETURN TO MY FAMILY.

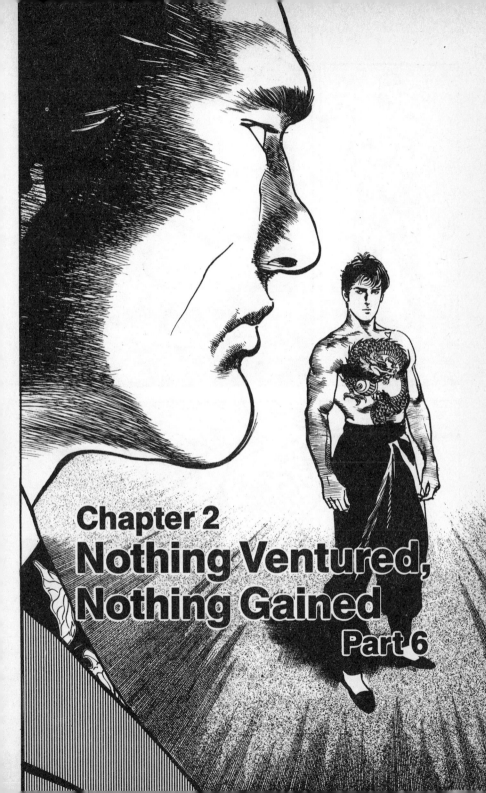

Chapter 2
Nothing Ventured, Nothing Gained
Part 6

TWNG

GRIT

HER HUSBAND MIGHT GET KILLED, AND YET SHE SEEMS SO VERY CALM. HOW DOES SHE DO IT?

IS IT BECAUSE SHE BELIEVES THAT HE IS THE BEST? ...THAT HE WILL NEVER LOSE?

MY HEART BEATS LIKE A JACKHAMMER. I CAN'T BE LIKE HER.

OSHU WAS ONCE THE STRONGEST PROFESSIONAL WRESTLER IN THE WORLD.

HE EMPLOYS THE FLYING-CROSS ATTACK, A DEADLY TECHNIQUE CALLED TOPÉ.

GRRRRRR

Waaaa

OSHU IS ARMED, AND HE HAS NO WEAKNESSES.

HOW CAN FREEMAN OVERCOME OSHU'S ADVANTAGES, NOT TO MENTION HIS SUPERIOR SIZE?

GLP

HI!!!!!

GRRRR

I... CAN'T HEAR... ANYTHING...

VERY... IMPRESSIVE... FREEMAN.

177

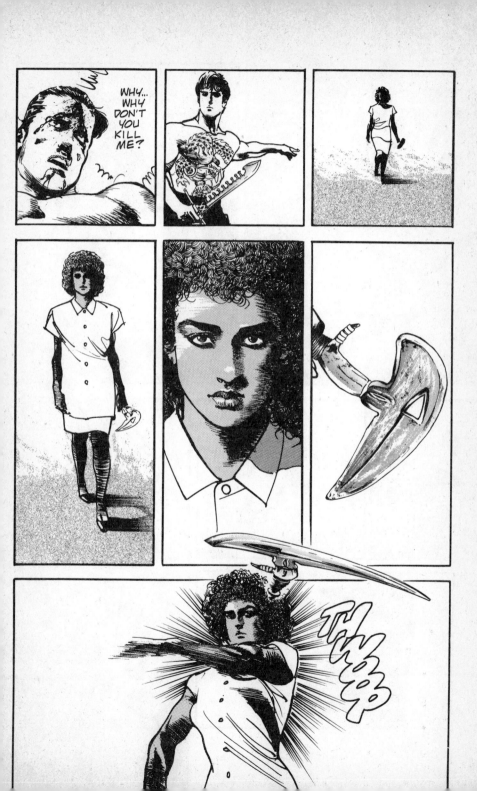

FWAAK

MY... FAMILY... PLEASE, MAKE THEM A PART OF YOUR OWN.

I HAVE BEEN... COMPLETELY DEFEATED.

AIEEE

182

IT'S OVER, DARK EYES.

END